A Christmas Carol

THE HEIRLOOM EDITION

A Christmas Carol

THE HEIRLOOM EDITION

BY CHARLES DICKENS

RETOLD BY JANE PARKER RESNICK

ILLUSTRATED BY CHRISTIAN BIRMINGHAM

RUNNING PRESS

PHILADELPHIA · LONDON

© 2002 by Running Press
Illustrations © 2000, 2002 by Christian Birmingham

All rights reserved under the Pan-American
and International Copyright Conventions

Printed in China

*This book may not be reproduced in whole or in part, in any form
or by any means, electronic or mechanical, including photocopying, recording,
or by any information storage and retrieval system now known or
hereafter invented, without written permission from the publisher.*

9   8   7   6   5   4   3   2
Digit on the right indicates the number of this printing

Library of Congress Cataloging-in-Publication Number 2002100485

ISBN 0-7624-1299-2

Interior and cover design by Bill Jones
Edited by Melissa Wagner
Typography: Minion, Bickham Script

This book may be ordered by mail from the publisher.
But try your bookstore first!

Published by Running Press Book Publishers
125 South Twenty-second Street
Philadelphia, Pennsylvania 19103-4399

Visit us on the web!
www.runningpress.com

CONTENTS

I have endeavored in this Ghostly little book,

to raise the Ghost of an Idea, which shall not

put my readers out of humor with themselves,

with each other, with the season, or with me.

May it haunt their house pleasantly,

and no one wish to lay it.

Their Faithful Friend and Servant, C.D.

December 1843

INTRODUCTION

When Charles Dickens wrote *A Christmas Carol* in 1843, he created a story for all ages, and for all time. His portrayal of the tight-fisted, mean-spirited mercenary who learns the true meaning of Christmas has such vitality that the name "Scrooge" has become a synonym for the ungenerous and unrelenting. More than one hundred fifty years later, no one wants to be called Scrooge. An extraordinary expression of the Christmas spirit, this brief novel is by turns jovial, nightmarish, and uplifting, but never pious or sentimental. *A Christmas Carol* is a fantasy grounded in reality, in which Dickens captures the worst and the best in human nature in ebullient, unforgettable prose.

CHAPTER ONE

Marley was dead to begin with. There is no doubt whatever about that. The register of his burial was signed by the clergyman, the undertaker, and the chief mourner. Scrooge signed it. Old Marley was dead as a doornail.

Scrooge knew he was dead? Of course he did. Scrooge and he were partners for I don't know how many years. Scrooge was his sole executor, his sole friend, and sole mourner. There is no doubt that Marley was dead. This must be distinctly understood, or nothing wonderful can come of the story I am going to relate.

Scrooge never painted out old Marley's name. There it stood years afterwards, above the warehouse door: Scrooge and Marley. Sometimes people called Scrooge Scrooge, and sometimes Marley, but he answered to both names, it was all the same to him.

Oh! but he was a tight fisted hand at the grind stone, Scrooge! A squeezing, wrenching, grasping, scraping, clutching, covetous old sinner! Hard and sharp as flint! Secret and solitary as an oyster. The cold within him froze his old features, nipped his pointed nose, shriveled his cheek, made his thin lips blue, and spoke out shrewdly in his grating voice. He carried his own low temperature always about him; he iced his office in the dog-days; and didn't thaw it one degree at Christmas.

External heat and cold had little influence on Scrooge. No warmth could warm him, nor wintry weather chill him. No wind that blew was bitterer than he, no falling snow was more intent upon its purpose, no pelting rain less open to entreaty.

Nobody ever stopped him in the street to say, with gladsome looks, "My dear Scrooge, how are you? When will you come to see me?" No beggars implored him to bestow a trifle, no children asked him what it was o'clock, no man or woman ever once in all his life inquired the way to such and such a place, of Scrooge. Even the blindmen's dogs appeared to know him; and when they saw him coming on, would tug their owners into doorways and up courts; and then would wag their tails as though they said, "no eye at all is better than an evil eye, dark master!"

Once upon a time—on Christmas Eve—old Scrooge sat busy in his counting-house. It was cold, bleak, biting weather, foggy withal, and he could hear the people in the court outside go wheezing up and down, beating their hands upon their breasts, and stamping their feet upon the pavement-stones to warm them. The city clocks had only just gone three, but it was quite dark already. It had not been light all day, and candles were flaring in the windows of the neighboring offices like ruddy smears upon the palpable brown air. The fog came pouring in at every chink and keyhole, and was so dense without that although the court was of the narrowest, the houses opposite were mere phantoms. To see the dingy cloud come drooping down, obscuring every-thing, one might have thought that Nature lived hard by, and was brewing on a large scale.

The door of Scrooge's counting-house was open that he might keep his eye upon his clerk, who in a dismal little cell beyond, a sort of tank, was copying letters.

Scrooge had a small fire, but the clerk's fire was so very much smaller that it looked like one coal. But he couldn't replenish it, for Scrooge kept the coal-box in his own room, and so surely as the clerk came in with the shovel, the master predicted that it would be necessary for them to part.

"A Merry Christmas, Uncle," cried a cheerful

voice. It was Scrooge's nephew, who came in the door unnoticed.

"Bah!" said Scrooge, "Humbug!" This nephew of Scrooge's was ruddy and handsome, all aglow from rapid walking.

"Christmas a humbug, uncle!" said Scrooge's nephew. "You don't mean that?"

"I do," said Scrooge. "Merry Christmas! What reason have you to be merry? You're poor enough."

"What right have you to be dismal?" returned his nephew gaily. "You're rich enough."

Scrooge, having no better answer ready, said, "Bah!" again, and followed it up with, "Humbug."

"Don't be cross," said the nephew.

"What else can I be, " returned the uncle, "when I live in such a world of fools as this? Merry Christmas! What's Christmas time to you but a time for paying bills without money, a time for finding your-self a year older, and not an hour richer? If I could work my will," said

Scrooge, indignantly, "every idiot who goes about with 'Merry Christmas' on his lips should be boiled with his own pudding and buried with a stake of holly through his heart. He should!"

"Uncle!" pleaded the nephew.

"Nephew!" returned the uncle, "Keep Christmas in your own way, and let me keep it in mine."

"Keep it!" repeated Scrooge's nephew. "But you don't keep it."

"Let me leave it alone, then," said Scrooge. "Much good it has ever done you!"

"There are many things from which I might have derived good, but from which I have not profited," returned the nephew. "I have always thought of Christmas as a good time—a kind, charitable, pleasant time; the only time when men open their shut-up hearts freely and think of people below them as if they really were fellow-passengers to the grave, and not another race of creatures bound on other journeys. Therefore, though it has never put a scrap of gold or

silver in my pocket, I believe that it has done me good, and will do me good; and I say, God bless it!"

The clerk in the rank involuntarily applauded.

"Let me hear another sound from you," said Scrooge, "and you'll keep your Christmas by losing your situation!"

"Don't be angry, uncle. Come! Dine with us tomorrow."

"Good afternoon," said Scrooge, ignoring the invitation.

"I want nothing from you. I ask nothing of you; why cannot we be friends?"

"Good afternoon," said Scrooge.

"I am sorry with all my heart to find you so resolute. But I have made the trial in homage to Christmas, so a Merry Christmas, uncle!"

His nephew left without an angry word, and as he departed, two other people came in. They were pleasant gentlemen, who stood with their hats off, in Scrooge's office.

"Scrooge and Marley's, I believe," said one of the gentlemen. "Have I the pleasure of addressing Mr. Scrooge, or Mr. Marley?"

"Mr. Marley has been dead these seven years," Scrooge replied. "He died seven years ago, this very night."

"We have no doubt his generosity is well represented by his surviving partner," said the gentleman.

Marley was well represented, all right, for they had been two kindred spirits. At the ominous word "generosity," Scrooge frowned.

"At this festive season, Mr. Scrooge," said the gentleman, "a few of us are endeavoring to raise a fund to buy the poor some meat and drink, and means of warmth. What shall I put you down for?"

"Nothing!" Scrooge replied. "Are there no prisons? No workhouses for these people?"

"Many can't go there; and many would rather die."

"If they would rather die," said Scrooge, "they had better do it, and decrease the surplus population. Besides, excuse me, I don't know that."

"But you might know it," observed the gentleman.

"It's not my business," Scrooge returned. "It's enough for a man to understand his own business, and not to interfere with other people's. Mine occupies me constantly. Good afternoon, gentlemen!"

Seeing that it would be useless to pursue their point, the gentlemen withdrew. Scrooge resumed his labors with an improved opinion of himself and a better temper than was usual.

Meanwhile, the fog and darkness thickened. The ancient church tower, whose old bell was always peeping slyly down at Scrooge out of a gothic window in the wall, became invisible, and struck the hours in the clouds, with tremulous vibrations afterwards as if its teeth were chattering in its frozen head. The piercing, biting cold became intense.

A boy, gnawed and numbed by the hungry cold, as bones are gnawed by dogs, stooped down at Scrooge's keyhole to regale him with a Christmas carol; but at the first sound of—

"God bless you merry gentlemen!" Scrooge seized the ruler with such energy of action that the singer fled in terror.

At length, the hour of shutting up the counting-house arrived. With an ill-will, Scrooge dismounted from his stool and tacitly admitted the fact to the expectant clerk in the tank, who instantly snuffed his candle out and put on his hat.

"You'll want all day tomorrow, I suppose?" said Scrooge.

"If quite convenient, sir."

"It's not convenient," said Scrooge, "and it's not fair. If I was to stop half-a-crown for it, you'd think yourself ill used. I'll be bound?"

The clerk smiled faintly.

"And yet," said Scrooge, "you don't think me ill used, when I pay a day's wages for no work."

The clerk observed that it was only once a year.

"A poor excuse for picking a man's pocket every twenty-fifth of December!" said Scrooge, buttoning his coat. "But I suppose you must have the whole day. Be here all the earlier the next morning!"

The clerk promised that he would, and Scrooge walked out with a growl. The office was closed in a twinkling; and the clerk, with the long ends of his white comforter dangling below his waist (for he wore no great-coat), went down with a slide on Cornhill, at the end of a lane of boys, twenty times, in honor of it being Christmas-eve, and then ran home to Camden Town as fast as he could to play blindman's-buff.

Scrooge took his melancholy dinner in his usual melancholy tavern; and having read all the newspapers, and beguiled the rest of the evening with his banker's book, went home to bed. He lived in chambers which had once belonged to his deceased partner. They were a gloomy suite of rooms, in a lowering pile of buildings, up a dilapidated yard. The yard was so dark that even Scrooge, who knew its every stone, was fain to grope with his hands. The fog and frost so hung about the old gateway of the house that it seemed as if the Genius of the Weather sat in mournful meditation on the threshold.

Now it is a fact that there was nothing at all particular about the knocker on the door, except that it was very large. It is also a fact that Scrooge had seen it night and morning during his whole residence in that place; also that Scrooge had as little of what is called fancy about him as any man in London. Let it also be remembered that Scrooge had not bestowed one thought on Marley since his last mention of his seven years' dead partner that afternoon. And then let any man explain to me, if he can, how it happened that Scrooge, having his key in the lock of the door, saw in the knocker, without its undergoing any intermediate process of change, not a knocker, but Marley's face.

Marley's face. It was not in impenetrable shadow as the other objects in the yard were, but had a dismal light about it. It was not angry, but looked at Scrooge as Marley used to look, with ghostly spectacles turned up upon its ghostly forehead. The hair was curiously stirred, as if by breath or hot-air, and though the eyes were wide open, they were perfectly motionless. That, and its livid color, made it horrible.

As Scrooge looked fixedly at this phenomenon, it was a knocker again.

To say that he was not startled, or that his blood was not conscious of a terrible sensation to which it had been a stranger from infancy, would be untrue. But he put his hand upon the key, turned it sturdily, walked in, and lighted his candle.

He did pause before he shut the door, and he did look cautiously behind it, as if he half expected to be terrified with the sight of Marley's pig-tail sticking out the back of the door. But there was nothing there except the screws and nuts that held the knocker on, so he said, "Pooh, pooh!" and closed it with a bang.

The sound resounded through the house like thunder. Scrooge was not a man to be frightened by echoes. He fastened the door and walked across the hall and up the stairs, slowly, too, trimming his candle as he went.

Up Scrooge went, not caring a button for the darkness of the staircase; darkness is cheap, and Scrooge liked it. But before he shut his heavy door, he walked through his rooms to see that all was right.

Sitting room, bedroom, lumber-room. All as they should be. Nobody under the table, nobody under the sofa, a small fire in the grate, spoon and basin ready, and the little saucepan of gruel (Scrooge had a cold in his head) upon the hob. Nobody under the bed, nobody in the closet, nobody in his dressing-gown which was hanging up against the wall.

Quite satisfied, he closed his door and locked

himself in—double-locked himself in, which was not his custom. Thus secured against surprise, he took off his cravat, put on his dressing-gown, slippers, and his night-cap, and sat down before the fire to take his gruel.

His gaze wandered and his glance rested upon a bell that hung in the room. It was with great astonishment, and with a strange, inexplicable dread, that he saw this bell begin to swing. It swung so softly in the outset that it scarcely made a sound, but soon it rang loudly, and so did every bell in the house.

This might have lasted half a minute, but it seemed an hour. They were succeeded by a clanking noise, deep down below, as if some person were dragging a heavy chain. Scrooge then remembered to have heard that ghosts in haunted houses were described as dragging chains.

The cellar-door flew open with a booming sound and then he heard the noise much louder, on the floors below; then coming up the stairs; then coming straight toward his door.

"It's humbug still!" said Scrooge. "I won't believe it."

His color changed, though, when without a pause it came on through the door and passed into the room before his eyes. Upon its coming, the dying flame in the fireplace leaped up, as though it cried, "I know him! Marley's Ghost!" and fell again.

The same face—the very same. Marley in his pig-tail, usual waistcoat, tights, and boots; the tassels on the latter bristling like his pig-tail and coat-skirts, and the hair upon his head. The chain he drew was clasped about his middle. It was long and wound about him like a tail, and it was made of cash-boxes, keys, padlocks, ledgers, deeds, and heavy purses wrought in steel. His body was transparent, so that Scrooge, observing him and looking through his waistcoat, could see the buttons on his coat behind.

Scrooge refused to believe it even now. Though he looked the phantom through and through, and saw it standing before him—though he felt the chilling influence of its death-cold eyes and marked the texture of the kerchief bound about its head and chin, which wrapper he had not observed before—he was still incredulous, and fought against his senses.

"How now!" said Scrooge, caustic and cold as ever. "What do you want with me?"

"Much"—Marley's voice, no doubt about it.

"Who are you?"

"In life I was your partner, Jacob Marley. You don't believe in me," observed the Ghost. "Do not

your senses convince you of my reality?"

"No," said Scrooge, "the littlest thing affects them. A slight disorder of the stomach makes them cheat. You may be an undigested bit of beef or a crumb of cheese. There's more of gravy than of grave about you, whatever you are!"

Scrooge was not much in the habit of cracking jokes. The truth is that he tried to be smart as a means of distracting his own attention and keeping down his terror, for the specter's voice disturbed the very marrow in his bones.

"You see this toothpick?" said Scrooge. "I have but to swallow this, and be for the rest of my days perse- cuted by a legion of gob- lins, all of my own cre- ation. Humbug, I tell you, humbug!"

At this, the spirit raised a frightful cry and shook its chain with such an appalling noise that Scrooge held on tight to his chair to save himself from falling in a swoon. But how much greater was his horror when the Phantom, taking off the band- age round its head as if it were too warm to wear indoors, dropped its lower jaw down upon its breast!

Scrooge fell upon his knees and clasped his hands before his face.

"Mercy!" he said. "Dreadful apparition, why do

you trouble me!"

"Do you believe in me or not?" replied the Ghost.

"I do," said Scrooge. "But why do spirits walk the earth, and why do they come to me?"

"It is required of every man," the Ghost returned, "that the spirit within him should walk abroad among his fellow men and travel far and wide, and if that spirit goes not forth in life, it is condemned to do so after death. It is doomed to wander through the world—oh, woe is me!— and witness what it cannot share, but might have shared on earth, and turned to happiness!"

Again the specter raised a cry, and shook its chain and wrung its shadowy hands.

"Why are you fettered?" said Scrooge, trembling.

"I wear the chain I forged in life," replied the Ghost. "I made it link by link—I girded it on of my own free will, and of my own free will I wore it. Is its pattern strange to you?"

Scrooge trembled more and more.

"Do you not know," pursued the Ghost, "the weight and length of the coil you bear yourself?"

"Jacob," he implored, "Old Jacob Marley, speak comfort to me."

"I have none to give," the Ghost replied. "I cannot stay, I cannot linger anywhere. My spirit never walked beyond our counting-house. Mark me!—in life my spirit never roved beyond the narrow limits of our money-changing hole, and weary journeys lie before me!"

"Seven years dead!" gasped Scrooge. "And traveling all the time?"

"The whole time," said the Ghost. "No rest, no peace. Incessant torture of remorse."

Then the Ghost set up another cry and clanked its chain hideously.

"Oh! Captive, bound, and double-ironed," cried the phantom. "Not to know that any Christian spirit working kindly in its little sphere, whatever that may be, will find its mortal life too short for its vast means of usefulness. Not to know that no space of regret can make amends for one life's opportunity misused! Yet such was I!"

"But you were always a good man of business, Jacob," faltered Scrooge, who now began to apply this to himself.

"Business! Mankind was my business. The common welfare was my business—charity, mercy, forbearance, and benevolence, were all my business. The dealings of my trade were but a drop of water in the ocean of my business!"

It held up its chain and flung it heavily upon the ground again.

"At this time of the year," the specter said, "I suffer most. Why did I walk through crowds of fellow beings with my eyes turned down, and never raise them to that blessed star which led the Wise Men to a poor abode? Were there no poor homes to which its light would have conducted me!"

Scrooge was much dismayed at what the specter said and began to quake exceedingly.

"Hear me!" cried the Ghost. "My time is nearly gone."

"I will," said Scrooge. "Don't be hard upon me, Jacob!"

"How it is that I appear before you in a shape that you can see, I may not tell. I am here to warn you, that you have yet a chance and hope of escaping my fate. A chance and hope of my procuring, Ebenezer."

"Oh, thank'ee," said Scrooge.

"You will be haunted," resumed the Ghost, "by three Spirits."

Scrooge's countenance fell.

"Is that the chance and hope you mentioned, Jacob?" he demanded in a faltering voice.

"Expect the first tomorrow when the bell tolls once. Expect the second on the next night at the same hour. The third upon the next night when the last stroke of twelve has ceased to vibrate. Look to see me no more, and, for your own sake, remember what has passed between us!"

When it had said these words, the specter took its wrapper and bound it round its head, as before. The apparition walked backward from Scrooge, and at every step it took the window opened a little, so that when the specter reached it, it was wide open.

Scrooge became sensible of noises in the air, incoherent sounds of lamentation and regret, wailings inexpressibly sorrowful and self-accusatory. The

specter joined in the mournful dirge, and then floated out upon the bleak, dark night.

Scrooge rushed to the window and looked out.

The air filled with phantoms wandering in restless
haste, and moaning as they went. Everyone wore
chains. Many had been personally known to Scrooge
in their lives. An old ghost with a monstrous iron
safe attached to its ankle cried at being unable to
assist a wretched woman with an infant, whom it
saw below, upon a doorstep. The misery with them
all was clearly that they sought to interfere, for good,
in human matters, and had lost the power forever.

The creatures disappeared. Scrooge closed the
window and examined the door by which the Ghost
had entered. It was double-locked. He tried to say:
"Humbug!" but stopped. He went straight to bed,
without undressing, and fell asleep upon the instant.

CHAPTER TWO

When Scrooge awoke, it was terribly dark and the chimes of a neighboring church struck the four quarters. So he listened for the hour.

To his great astonishment the heavy bell tolled twelve. Twelve! It was past two when he went to bed. The clock was wrong. An icicle must have got into the works. Twelve!

"Why, it isn't possible," said Scrooge, "that I can have slept through a whole day and into another night."

The idea being an alarming one, he scrambled out of bed to the window. But all he could make out was that it was still foggy and extremely cold and there were no people running to and fro on the street. Scrooge went to bed again, and thought and thought it over and could make nothing of it. The more he thought, the more perplexed he was. Marley's ghost bothered him exceedingly. Every time he resolved within himself that it was all a dream, his mind flew back again, like a strong spring released, to its first position. "Was it a dream or not?"

Scrooge lay in this state until the chimes had gone three quarters more when he remembered, on a sudden, that the Ghost had warned him of a visitation when the bell tolled one. He waited. The quarter was interminably long.

"Ding, dong!"

"A quarter past," said Scrooge, counting.

"Ding, dong!"

"Half past!" said Scrooge.

"Ding, dong!"

"A quarter to it," said Scrooge.

"Ding, dong!"

"The hour itself," said Scrooge, triumphantly, "and nothing else!"

He spoke before the hour bell sounded, which it now did with a deep, dull, hollow, melancholy ONE. Light flashed up in the room upon the instant, and the curtains of his bed were drawn.

The curtains of his bed were drawn aside, I tell you, by a hand. And Scrooge found himself face to face with the unearthly visitor who drew them. It was a strange figure, like a child, yet not so like a child as like an old man viewed through some supernatural medium, which gave him the appearance of having receded from view and being diminished in a

would be itself again, distinct and clear.

"Are you the Spirit whose coming was foretold to me?" asked Scrooge.

"I am!" The voice was soft and gentle.

"Who and what are you?"

"I am the Ghost of Christmas Past."

"Long past?" inquired Scrooge.

"No. Your past."

Perhaps Scrooge could not have told anybody why, but he had a special desire to see the Spirit in his cap, and begged him to be covered.

"What!" exclaimed the Ghost, "would you so soon put out, with worldly hands, the light I give?"

Scrooge reverently disclaimed all intention to offend and then made bold to inquire what business brought him there.

"Your welfare!" said the Ghost. "Your reclamation! Take heed!"

It put out its strong hand and clasped Scrooge gently by the arm. "Rise! And walk with me!"

As these words were spoken, they passed through the wall, and stood upon an open country road. The city and fog completely vanished, for it was a clear winter day with snow upon the ground.

"Good Heavens!" said Scrooge, clasping his hands together, as he looked about him. "I was bred in this place. I was a boy here!" He was conscious of a thousand thoughts and hopes and joys long forgotten!

They walked along the road; Scrooge recognizing every gate, and post, and tree. Some ponies now were seen trotting towards them with boys upon their backs, who shouted to each other in great spirits until the fields were so full of merry music, that

child's proportions. Its hair was white as if with age, and yet the face had not a wrinkle in it. It wore a tunic of the purest white, and round its waist was bound a lustrous belt, the sheen of which was beautiful. But the strangest thing about it was that from the crown of its head there sprung a bright, clear jet of light, and under its arm was a cap which was doubtless used as a great extinguisher.

Even this, though, when Scrooge looked at it with increasing steadiness, was not its strangest quality. For the figure fluctuated in distinctness, being now a thing with one arm, now with one leg, now with twenty legs, now a pair of legs without a head, now a head without a body; of which dissolving parts, no outline would be visible in the dense gloom wherein they melted away. And in the wonder of this, it the crisp air laughed to hear it.

"These are but shadows of things that have been," said the Ghost. "They have no consciousness of us."

The jocund travelers came nearer and Scrooge knew every one. Why was he rejoiced beyond all bounds to see them? Why was he filled with gladness when he heard them say, "Merry Christmas?" What was "Merry Christmas" to Scrooge? What good had it ever done to him?

"That school is not quite deserted," said the Ghost. "A solitary child, neglected by his friends, is left there still."

Scrooge said he knew it. And he sobbed.

They left the road and approached the school, an ancient mansion, crumbling with disrepair. They entered the great cold hall of the building. There was an earthy savor in the air, a chilly bareness in the place, which associated itself somehow with too much getting up by candlelight, and not too much to eat.

They walked, the Ghost and Scrooge, to a room at the back of the house, a long, bare, melancholy room lined with desks. At one of these, a lonely boy was reading near a feeble fire, and Scrooge sat down upon a seat and wept to see his poor forgotten self as he had used to be.

Not a latent echo in the house, not a squeak or scuffling from the mice behind the paneling, not a drip from the half-thawed water-spout in the dull yard behind, not a sigh among the leafless boughs of one despondent poplar, not the idle swinging of an empty store-house door— no, not a clicking in the fire, but fell upon the heart of Scrooge with a soften-

ing influence, and gave a freer passage to his tears.

"Poor boy!" Scrooge exclaimed and cried again. "I wish," Scrooge muttered, drying his eyes with his cuff. "But it's too late now."

"What is the matter?" asked the Spirit.

"Nothing," said Scrooge. "Nothing. There was a boy singing a Christmas carol at my door last night. I should liked to have given him something. That's all."

The Ghost smiled thoughtfully, and waved its hand saying, "Let us see another Christmas!"

Scrooge's former self grew larger at the words, and the room became darker and more dirty. There he was, alone again, when all the other boys had gone home for the holidays.

He was not reading now, but walking up and down despairingly. Scrooge looked at the Ghost, and with a mournful shaking of his head, glanced anxiously towards the door.

It opened, and a little girl, much younger than the boy, came darting in, and putting her arms about his neck and kissing him, addressed him as her "Dear, dear brother."

"I have come to bring you home!" said the child, clapping her hands and laughing.

"Home, little Fan?" returned the boy.

"Yes!" said the child, brimful of glee. "Home, for good, for ever and ever. Father is so much kinder than he used to be, that home's like Heaven! He spoke so gently to me one night that I asked him once more if you might come home, and he said yes. He sent me in a coach to bring you home and you're never to come back here. But first, we're to be together all the Christmas long, and have the merriest time."

"You are quite a woman, little Fan!" exclaimed the boy.

She stood on tiptoe to embrace him. Then she began to drag him, in her childish eagerness, towards the door; and he, nothing loathe to go, accompanied her.

"Always a delicate creature," said the Ghost.

"But she had a large heart!"

"So she had," cried Scrooge. "You're right. I'll not gainsay it, Spirit!"

"She died a woman," said the Ghost, "and had, as I think, children."

"One child," Scrooge returned.

"True," said the Ghost. "Your nephew!"

Scrooge seemed uneasy in his mind and answered briefly, "Yes."

Although they had but that moment left the school behind them, they were now in the busy thoroughfares of a city. It was made plain enough by the dressing of the shops that here, too, it was Christmas time again, but it was evening, and the streets were lighted up.

The Ghost stopped at a certain warehouse door, and asked Scrooge if he knew it.

"Knew it!" said Scrooge. "Was I apprenticed here?"

They went in. At the sight of an old gentleman in a Welsh wig, sitting behind such a high desk, Scrooge cried to great excitement.

"Why it's old Fezziwig! Bless his heart; it's Fezziwig alive again!"

Old Fezziwig laid down his pen, looked up at the clock, and called out in a rich, jovial voice: "Yo ho, there! Ebenezer! Dick!"

Scrooge's former self, now grown a young man, came briskly in, accompanied by his fellow-'prentice.

"Dick Wilkins!" said Scrooge to the Ghost. "He was very much attached to me, was Dick. Poor Dick! Dear!"

"Yo ho, my boys!" said Fezziwig. "No more work tonight. Christmas Eve, Ebenezer! Let's have the shutters up. Hilli-ho, my lads! Clear away, and let's have lots of room here!"

In came a fiddler with a music-book, and went up to the lofty desk, and made an orchestra of it, and tuned like fifty stomach-aches. In came Mrs. Fezziwig, one vast substantial smile. In came the three Miss Fezziwigs, beaming and lovable. In came the six young followers whose hearts they broke. In came all the young men and women employed in the business. In came the housemaid, with her cousin, the baker. In came the cook, with her brother's particular friend, the milkman. In came the boy from over the way, who was suspected of not having board enough from his master, trying to hide himself behind the girl from next door, who was proved to have had her ears pulled by her Mistress. In they all came, one after another, some shyly, some boldly, some gracefully, some awkwardly, some pushing, some pulling; in they all came, any-how and everyhow. Away they all went, twenty couples at once, hands half round and back again the other way, down the middle and up again, round and round in various stages of affectionate grouping. There were more dances, and they dined on cakes and roasts and mince pies, and they drank more than plenty of beer.

When the clock struck eleven, this domestic ball broke up. Mr. and Mrs. Fezziwig took their stations, one on either side the door, and shaking hands with every person, wished him or her a Merry Christmas until the cheerful voices died away. At last, they wished the two 'prentices a warm, Merry Christmas and the lads were left to their beds.

During the whole of this time, Scrooge had acted like a man out of his wits. His heart and soul were in the scene and with his former self. He recalled every-thing, enjoyed everything, and underwent the strangest agitation. It was not until now that he remembered the Ghost, and became con-scious that it was looking full upon him, while the light upon its head burnt very clear.

"A small matter," said the Ghost, "to make these silly folks so full of grati-tude."

"Small!" echoed Scrooge.

"Why! Is it not?" the Ghost questioned him. "Fezziwig has spent but a few pounds of your mortal money for his party. Is that so much that he deserves great praise?"

"It isn't that," said Scrooge, heated by the remark and speaking unconsciously like his former, not his latter, self. "He has the power to render us happy or unhappy; to make our service a pleasure or a toil. Say that his power lies in words and looks, in things so slight and insignificant that it is impossible to add and count 'em up; what then? The happiness he gives is quite as great as if it cost a fortune. "

He felt the Spirit's glance and stopped.

"What is the matter? " asked the Ghost.

"I should like to be able to say a word or two to my clerk just now! " said Scrooge. "That's all. "

His former self turned down the lamps and Scrooge and the Ghost again stood in the open air.

"My time grows short, " observed the Spirit. "Quick! "

This was not addressed to Scrooge, but it produced an immediate effect. For again Scrooge saw himself. He was older now, a man in the prime of life. His face had not the harsh and rigid lines of later years, but it had begun to wear the signs of care and avarice. There was an eager, greedy, restless motion in his eye which showed the passion that had taken root.

He was not alone, but sat by a fair young girl in a mourning dress, in whose eyes there were tears which sparkled in the light that shone out of the Ghost of Christmas past.

"Our contract is an old one, " she said. "It was made when we were both poor and content to be so, until, in good season, we could improve our fortune by our patient industry. You are changed. I have seen your nobler aspirations fall off one by one, until the master-passion, gain, engrosses you. When our contract was made you were another man. "

"I was a boy, " he said impatiently.

"How often and how keenly I have thought of this, I will not say. It is enough that I have thought of it, and can release you. "

"Have I ever sought release? "

"In words, no. Never. "

"In what, then?"

"In an altered spirit; in another atmosphere of life; another hope as its great end. In everything that made my love of any worth in your sight. If this contract had never been between us, " said the girl, "tell me, would you seek me out now? Ah, no! "

He seemed to yield to the justice of this supposition, in spite of himself. But he said, with a struggle, "You think not? "

"I would gladly think otherwise if I could, " she answered. "But if you were free today, can even I believe that you would choose a dowerless girl, you who weigh everything by gain. Or, if you chose her, in a moment of false to your guiding principle, do I not know that your repentance and regret would surely follow? I do, and I release you. May you be happy in the life you have chosen! "

She left him, and they parted.

"Spirit! " said Scrooge, "Show me no more! Conduct me home. Why do you delight to torture me? "

"One shadow more! " exclaimed the Ghost.

"No more!' cried Scrooge. "No more. I don't wish to see it. Show me no more! "

But the relentless Ghost pinioned him in both his arms, and forced him to observe what happened next.

They were in another scene and place, a room, not large or handsome, but full of comfort. Near the fire sat a beautiful young girl, so like the last that Scrooge believed it was the same, until he saw her, now a comely matron, sitting opposite her daughter. The noise in this room was tumultuous, for there were more children there than Scrooge could count, all cavorting about gaily. The mother and daughter laughed heartily, enjoying themselves very much.

Then a knocking at the door was heard and a rush immediately ensued to greet the father, who came home laden with Christmas toys and presents. What joy and ecstasy!

And now Scrooge looked on more attentively than ever, when the master of the house, having his daughters leaning fondly on him, sat down with her and her mother at his own fireside, and when he thought that such another creature, quite as lovely, might have called him father, and been a spring-time in the haggard winter of his life, his sight grew very dim indeed.

"Belle," said the husband, "I saw an old friend of yours this afternoon."

"Who was that?" she asked.

"Mr. Scrooge. I passed his office window and saw him inside. His partner lies upon the point of death, I hear, and there he sat alone. Quite alone in the world, I do believe."

"Spirit!" said Scrooge, in a broken voice, "Remove me from this place."

"I told you these were shadows of the things that have been," said the Ghost. "That they are what they are, do not blame me!"

"Remove me!" Scrooge exclaimed. "I cannot bear it!"

He turned upon the Ghost, and seeing that it looked upon his with a face in which in some strange way there were fragments of all the faces it had shown him, wrestled with it.

"Leave me! Haunt me no longer!"

In the struggle, Scrooge observed that the Ghost's light was burning high and bright, and dimly connecting that with its influence over him, he seized the extinguisher-cap, and by a sudden action pressed it down upon its head. The Spirit dropped beneath it, so that the extinguisher covered its whole form; but though Scrooge pressed it down, he could not hide the light which streamed from under it in an unbroken flood upon the ground.

He was conscious of being exhausted, and overcome by an irresistible drowsiness and of being in his own bedroom. He had barely time to reel to bed, before he sank into a heavy sleep.

CHAPTER THREE

*A*waking in the middle of a prodigiously tough snore, and sitting up in bed to get his thoughts together, Scrooge had no occasion to be told that the bell was again upon the stroke of One. He felt that he was restored to consciousness in the nick of time, for the especial purpose of holding a conference with the second messenger dispatched to him through Jacob Marley's intervention. Now, being prepared for almost anything, he was still not prepared for nothing and, consequently, when the bell struck one and no shape appeared, he was taken with a violent fit of trembling. Five, ten minutes, a quarter of an hour went by, yet nothing came. All this time, he lay upon his bed, the very core and center of a blaze of ruddy light which streamed upon it when the clock proclaimed the hour, and which being only light, was more alarming than a dozen ghosts, as he was powerless to make out what it meant. At last, however, he began to think that the source of the ghostly light might be in the adjoining room, from whence it seemed to shine. So, tremulously, he got up and shuffled to the door.

The moment Scrooge's hand was on the lock, a strange voice called him by his name, and bade him enter. He obeyed.

It was his own room. There was no doubt about that. But it had undergone a surprising transformation. The walls and ceiling were so hung with living green that it looked a perfect grove, from every part of which bright gleaming berries glistened. The crisp leaves of holly, mistletoe, and ivy reflected back the light, as if so many little mirrors had been scattered there, and a mighty blaze went roaring up the chimney. Heaped up on the floor, to form a kind of throne, were turkeys, geese, game, poultry, brawn, great joints of meat, suckling pigs, long wreaths of sausages, mince pies, plum puddings, barrels of oysters, red hot chestnuts, cherry cheeked apples, juicy oranges, luscious pears, immense twelfth cakes, and seething bowls of punch that made the chamber dim with their delicious steam. Upon this couch there sat a jolly giant, glorious to see, who bore a glowing torch in the shape not unlike Plenty's horn, and held it up to shed its light to Scrooge as he came peeping round the door.

"Come in!" exclaimed the Ghost. "Come in!

And know me better, man!"

Scrooge entered timidly and hung his head before this Spirit. He was not the stubborn Scrooge he had been, and though the Spirit's eyes were clear and kind, he did not like to meet them.

"I am the Ghost of Christmas Present," said the Spirit. "Look upon me!"

Scrooge reverently did so. It was clothed in one simple green robe, bordered with white fur. This garment hung so loosely on the figure that its capacious breast was bare. Its feet were also bare, and on its head it wore a holly wreath, set with shining icicles. Its dark brown curls were long and free, free as its genial face, its sparkling eyes, its open hand, its cheery voice, its unconstrained demeanor, and its joyful air.

The Ghost of Christmas Present rose.

"Spirit," said Scrooge submissively, "conduct me where you wish. I went forth last night on compulsion, and I learned a lesson which is working now. Tonight, if you have aught to reach me, let me profit by it."

"Touch my robe!"

Scrooge did as he was told, and held it fast.

Holly, mistletoe, red berries, ivy, turkeys, geese, game, poultry, brawn, meat, pigs, sausages, oysters, pies, pudding, fruit, and punch—all vanished instantly. So did the room, the fire, the ruddy glow, the hour of night, and they stood in the city streets on Christmas morning, where people made a rough music scraping the snow from the pavement in front of their dwellings and from the tops of their houses, whence it was mad delight to the boys to see it come plumping down into the road below and splitting into artificial little snow-storms.

The house fronts looked black enough, and the windows blacker, contrasting with the smooth white sheet of snow upon the roofs and with the dirtier snow upon the ground. The sky was gloomy and the streets were choked with a dingy mist as if all the chimneys in Great Britain were blasting away at once. There was nothing cheerful in the climate or the town, and yet there was an air of cheerfulness abroad that the clearest summer air and brightest sun might have endeavored to diffuse in vain.

For the people who were shoveling away on the housetops were jovial and full of glee, calling out to one another. The poulterers' shops were still half open, and

30

the fruiterers' were radiant in their glory. There were potbellied baskets of chestnuts, pyramids of pears and apples, and bunches of grapes dangling from conspicuous hooks.

The Grocers! Oh, the Grocers! were nearly closed, but through the gaps between the shutters such glimpses of raisins, almonds, and candied fruits, so caked and spotted with molten sugar as to make the coldest lookers-on feel faint. The customers were all eager in the hopeful promise of the day that they tumbled against each other at the door.

But soon the steeples called good people all to church, and away they came, flocking through the streets in their best clothes and gayest faces. And at the same time there emerged from scores of by-lanes and nameless streets innumerable people carrying their dinners to the bakers' shops. The sight of these poor revelers interested the Spirit very much, for he stood with Scrooge beside him in a baker's doorway, and sprinkled incense on their dinners from his torch. And it was a very uncommon kind of torch, for at times, when there were angry words between some dinner carriers who had jostled each other, he shed a few drops of water on them from it and their good humor was restored directly. For they said it was a shame to quarrel upon Christmas Day. And so it was! God love it, so it was!

"Is there a peculiar flavor in what you sprinkle from your torch?" asked Scrooge.

"There is. My own."

"Would it apply to any kind of dinner on this day?"

"To any kindly given. To a poor one most."

"Why to a poor one most?" asked Scrooge.

"Because it needs it most."

Then they went on into the suburbs of the town. Perhaps it was the Spirit's own kind, generous nature, and his sympathy with all poor men, that led him straight to Scrooge's clerk's. For there he went, and took Scrooge with him, holding to his robe, and on the threshold of the door, the Spirit stopped to bless Bob Cratchit's dwelling with the sprinkling of his torch. Think of that! The Ghost of Christmas Present blessed Bob's poor four-roomed house!

Then up rose Mrs. Cratchit dressed poorly in a twice-turned gown, but brave in ribbons which are cheap but make a goodly show. She laid the cloth, assisted by Belinda Cratchit, second of her daughters, while Master Peter Cratchit stood proudly with his thin neck swallowed in his father's shirt. And now two smaller Cratchits, boy and girl, came tearing in, screaming that outside the baker's they had smelt the goose and known it for their own. Basking in luxurious thoughts of sage and onion, these young Cratchits danced about the table and exalted Master Peter Cratchit to the skies, while he (not proud, although his collars nearly choked him) blew the fire until the slow potatoes, bubbling up, knocked loudly at the saucepan-lid to be let out and peeled.

"Where is your father then," said Mrs. Cratchit. "And your brother, Tiny Tim, and Martha, your sister?"

"Here's Martha!" said a girl, appearing as she spoke.

"How late you are, my dear!" said Mrs. Cratchit, kissing her a dozen times.

"We'd still a deal of work to do this morning,

mother," replied the girl.

"Sit down before the fire, dear, and have a warm," said Mrs. Cratchit.

"No! There's father coming," cried the two young Cratchits. "Hide Martha, hide!"

So Martha hid herself, and in came Bob, the father, his thread-bare clothes darned up and brushed to look seasonable, and Tiny Tim upon his shoulder. Alas for Tiny Tim, he bore a little crutch, and his limbs supported by an iron frame!

"Where's our Martha?" cried Bob Cratchit looking around.

"Not coming," said Mrs. Cratchit.

"Not coming upon Christmas Day!" said Bob, with a sudden declension in his high spirits.

Martha didn't like to see him disappointed, even if it were only in joke; she came out from behind the door and ran into his arms.

Master Peter and the two young Cratchits went to fetch the goose, with which they soon returned in high procession.

Such a bustle ensued that you might have thought a goose the rarest of all birds, and in truth it was something like it in that house. Mrs. Cratchit made the gravy sizzling hot; Master Peter mashed the pota-toes; Miss Belinda sweetened the applesauce. Bob took Tiny Tim beside him in a tiny corner at the table. At last everyone sat down and grace was said. It was succeeded by a breathless pause, as Mrs. Cratchit prepared to plunge the carving knife into the breast of the goose. But when she did, and when the long expected gush of stuffing issued forth, one murmur of delight arose all round the board, and even Tiny Tim, excited by the two young Cratchits, beat on the table and feebly cried, "Hurrah!"

There never was such a goose. Bob said he didn't believe there ever was such a goose cooked. Eked out by the applesauce and mashed potatoes, it was a sufficient dinner for the whole family. Then Mrs. Cratchit disappeared into the kitchen and emerged, smiling proudly, with the pudding, like a speckled cannon-ball, blazing in ignited brandy with Christmas holly stuck into the top.

At last the dinner was all done and the Cratchit family drew round the hearth. Bob concocted a hot drink of lemon and gin and passed the jug to everyone while chestnuts crackled on the fire.

Bob proposed a toast:

"A Merry Christmas to us all, my dears. God bless us!"

Which all the family echoed.

"God bless us every one!" said Tiny Tim, the last of all.

He sat close to his father's side, upon his stool. Bob held his withered little hand in his, as if he loved the child and wished to keep him by his side, and dreaded that he might be taken from him.

"Spirit," said Scrooge, with an interest he had never felt before, "tell me if Tiny Tim will live."

"I see a vacant seat," replied the Ghost, "in the chimney corner, and a crutch without an owner, carefully preserved. If these shadows remain unaltered by the future, the child will die."

"No!" said Scrooge. "Oh no, kind Spirit! Say he will be spared."

"If these shadows remain unaltered by the future,

none other of my race," returned the Ghost, "will find him here. What then? If he be like to die, he had better do it, and decrease the surplus population."

Scrooge hung his head to hear his own words quoted by the spirit, and was overcome with penitence and grief.

"Man," said the Ghost, "if man you be in heart, not adamant, forbear that wicked cant until you have discovered what the surplus is, and where it is. Will you decide what men shall live, what men shall die? It may be that in the sight of Heaven you are more worthless and less fit to live than millions like this poor man's child."

Scrooge bent before the Ghost's rebuke, and trembling, cast his eyes upon the ground. But he raised them speedily, on hearing his own name.

"Mr. Scrooge!" said Bob. "I'll give you Mr. Scrooge, the founder of the feast!"

"The founder of the feast indeed!" cried Mrs. Cratchit, reddening. "I wish I had him here. I'd give him a piece of my mind to feast upon, and I hope he'd have a good appetite for it."

"My dear," said Bob, "the children; Christmas Day."

"It should be Christmas Day, I am sure," said she, "on which one drinks the health of such an odious, stingy, hard, unfeeling man as Mr. Scrooge. You know he is, Robert! Nobody knows it better than you do, poor fellow!"

"My dear," was Bob's mild answer, "Christmas Day."

"I'll drink his health for your sake and the Day's," said Mrs. Cratchit, "not for his. Long life to him! A Merry Christmas and a happy New Year!—He'll be merry and happy, I have no doubt!"

The children drank the toast after her. It was the first of their proceedings which had no heartiness in it. Tiny Tim drank it last of all, but he didn't care two pence for it. Scrooge was the ogre of the family. His name cast a shadow on the party, which was not dispelled for several minutes.

After it passed away, they were ten times merrier than before, from the mere relief of Scrooge the Baleful being done with. All this time the chestnuts and the jug went round, and bye and bye they had a song from Tiny Tim about a lost child traveling in the snow. He had a plaintive little voice and sang it very well indeed.

There was nothing of high mark in this. They were not a handsome family, nor well off. But they were happy, grateful, pleased with one another, and contented. And when they faded from sight and looked happier yet in the bright sprinklings of the Spirit's torch at parting, Scrooge had his eye upon them, and especially on Tiny Tim, until the last.

By this time it was getting dark and snowing heavily, and as Scrooge and the Spirit went along the streets, the brightness of the fires in kitchens and parlors was wonderful. Here, the blaze showed preparations for a dinner, with hot plates baking through before the fire. There, the children of the house were running out to meet their married sisters, brothers, cousins, and be the first to greet them.

If you had judged from the numbers of people on their way to friendly gatherings, you might have thought that no one was at home to give them welcome when they got there. Blessings on it, how the Ghost exulted! How it bared its breast and opened its capacious palm, and floated on, outpouring with a generous hand its bright and harmless mirth on everything within its reach!

And now, without a word of warning from the Ghost, they stood upon a bleak and desert moor, where monstrous masses of rude stone were cast about as though it were the burial-place of giants. Nothing grew on the icy ground but moss and coarse grass. Down in the west the setting sun had left a streak of fiery red which glared upon the desolation for an instant like a sullen eye, and frowning lower, lower, lower yet, was lost in the thick gloom of darkest night.

"What place is this?" asked Scrooge.

"A place where miners live, who labor in the bowels of the earth," returned the spirit. "But they know me. See!"

A light shone through the window of a hut, and swiftly they advanced towards it. Passing through the wall of mud and stone, they found a cheerful company assembled round a glowing fire. An old, old man and woman, with their children and their children's children, and another generation beyond that, all decked out gaily in their holiday attire. The old man, in a voice that seldom rose above the howling of the wind, was singing them an old Christmas song, and from time to time they all joined in the chorus.

The Spirit did not tarry here, but bade Scrooge hold his robe, and passing on above the moor, sped out to sea. To Scrooge's horror, looking back, he saw the last of the land, a frightful range of rocks behind them, and his ears were deafened by the thundering of water as it rolled, and roared, and raged.

Built upon a dismal reef of sunken rocks, there

stood a solitary lighthouse. Great heaps of seaweed clung to its base, and storm birds rose and fell about it, like the waves they skimmed.

But even here, two men who watched the light had made a fire that, through the loophole in the thick stone wall, shed out a ray of brightness on the awful sea. Joining their worn hands over the rough table at which they sat, they wished each other Merry Christmas in their can of grog.

Again the Ghost sped on, above the black and heaving sea, until they lighted on a ship. They stood beside the helmsman at the wheel, the look-out in the bow, the officers who had the watch; dark, ghostly figures in their several stations; but every man among them hummed a Christmas tune, or had a Christmas thought, or spoke to his companion of some past Christmas Day. Every man on board had a kinder word for another on that day than on any day in the year, and had remembered those he cared for at a distance, and had known that they delighted to remember him.

It was a great surprise to Scrooge, while listening to the moaning of the wind, to hear a loud and hearty laugh. It was an even greater surprise to Scrooge to recognize it as his own nephew's, and to find himself in a bright gleaming room with the Spirit standing smiling by his side, and looking at that same nephew with approving affability!

"Ha, ha!" laughed Scrooge's nephew. "Ha, ha, ha!" If you should happen, by an unlikely chance, to know a man more blest in a laugh than Scrooge's nephew, all I can say is, I should like to know him, too. Scrooge's niece, by marriage, laughed as heartily as his nephew. And their assembled friends being a bit behind-hand, roared out lustily.

"Ha, ha! Ha, ha, ha, ha!"

"He said that Christmas was a humbug, as I live!" cried Scrooge's nephew. "He believed it, too!"

"More shame for him, Fred!" said Scrooge's niece, indignantly.

She was exceedingly pretty, with a dimpled, capital face. Oh, perfectly satisfactory!

"He's a comical old fellow," said Scrooge's nephew, "that's the truth, and not so pleasant as he might be. However, his offenses carry their own punishment, and I have nothing to say against him."

"I'm sure he is very rich, Fred," hinted Scrooge's niece.

"What of that, my dear!" said Scrooge's nephew. "His wealth is of no use to him. He doesn't do any good with it. He doesn't make himself comfortable with it. He hasn't the satisfaction of thinking—ha, ha, ha—that he is ever going to benefit us with it."

"I have no patience with him," observed Scrooge's niece.

"I have!" said Scrooge's nephew. "I am sorry for him; I couldn't be angry with him if I tried. Who suffers by his ill whims! Himself, always. Here he takes it into his head to dislike us, and he won't come and dine with us. What's the consequence? He loses some pleasant moments, which could do him no harm. I mean to give him the same chance every year, whether he likes it or not, for I pity him. He may rail at Christmas till he dies, but he can't help thinking better of it—I defy him—if he finds me going there year after year and saying 'Uncle

Scrooge, how are you?' If it only puts him in a mind to leave his poor clerk fifty pounds, that's something; and I think I shook him yesterday."

It was their turn to laugh now, at the notion of his shaking Scrooge. But being good-natured and not much caring what they laughed at, he encouraged them in their merriment and passed the bottle, joyously.

After tea, they had some music. The songs that Scrooge's niece played upon the harp reminded him of tunes he had known in his childhood. When this strain of music sounded, all the things the Ghost of Christmas Past had shown Scrooge came upon his mind; he softened more and more; and thought that if he could have listened to it often, years ago, he might have cultivated the kindnesses of life for his own happiness, with his own hands.

The evening then progressed to games and there might have been twenty people there, young and old, but they all played, and so did Scrooge. Wholly caught up in what was going on, and forgetting that his voice made no sound in their ears, he sometimes came out with answers to the games' questions, and often guessed right, too.

The Ghost was greatly pleased to find him in this mood, and looked upon him with such favor that Scrooge begged like a boy to be allowed to stay until the guests departed. But this the Spirit said could not be done, and without warning, he and the Spirit were again upon their travels.

Much they saw, and far they went, and many homes they visited, but always with a happy end. The Spirit stood beside sick beds, and they were cheerful; by struggling men, and they were patient in their greater hope; by poverty, and it was rich. In almshouse, hospital, and jail, in misery's every refuge, where vain man in his little brief authority had not made fast the door and barred the Spirit out, he left his blessing and taught Scrooge his precepts.

It was a long night, if it were only a night. It was strange, too, that the Ghost grew older, clearly older, and his hair grew gray. Scrooge could not help but notice.

"Are spirits' lives so short?" asked Scrooge.

"My life upon this globe is very brief," replied the Ghost. "It ends tonight."

"Tonight!" cried Scrooge.

"Tonight at midnight. Hark! The time is drawing near."

The chimes were ringing the three quarters past eleven at the moment.

"Forgive me if I am not justified in what I ask," said Scrooge, looking intently at the Spirit's robe, "but I see something strange protruding from your skirts."

"Oh, Man! Look here," was the Spirit's sorrowful reply.

From the foldings of its robe, it brought two children, wretched, ragged, frightful, miserable. Where graceful youth should have filled their features out, a stale and shriveled hand, like that of age, had pinched and twisted them and pulled them into shreds. Where angels might have sat enthroned, devils lurked and glared out menacing. Scrooge started back, appalled.

"Spirit! Are they yours?" He could say no more.

"They are Man's," said the Spirit. "This boy is Ignorance. This girl is Want."

"Have they no refuge or resource?" cried Scrooge.

"Are there no prisons?" said the Spirit, turning on him for the last time with his own words. "Are there no workhouses?"

The bell struck twelve.

Scrooge looked about him for the Ghost, and saw it not. As the last stroke ceased to vibrate, he remembered the prediction of old Jacob Marley, and lifting up his eyes beheld a solemn Phantom, draped and hooded, coming like a mist along the ground towards him.

CHAPTER FOUR

The Phantom slowly, gravely, silently, approached. When it came near him, Scrooge bent down upon his knee, for in the very air through which this Spirit moved it seemed to scatter gloom and mystery.

It was shrouded in a deep black garment which concealed its head, its face, its form, and left nothing of it visible, save one outstretched hand. But for this, it would have been difficult to separate its figure from the darkness which surrounded it.

When it came beside Scrooge, its mysterious presence filled him with dread. The Spirit neither spoke nor moved.

"I am in the presence of the Ghost of Christmas Yet to Come?" said Scrooge.

The Spirit answered not, but pointed onward.

"You are about to show me shadows of things that have not happened, but will happen in the time before us," Scrooge pursued. "Is that so, Spirit?"

The garment moved slightly as if the Spirit had inclined its head.

Although well used to ghostly company by now, Scrooge feared this silent shape so much that his legs trembled and he could hardly stand when he prepared to follow it. It thrilled him with a vague uncertain horror to know that behind the dusky shroud there were ghostly eyes intently fixed upon him, while he could see nothing but a spectral hand.

"Ghost of the future!" he exclaimed, "I fear you more than any Specter I have seen. But as I know your purpose is to do me good, and as I hope to live to be another man from what I was, I am prepared to bear your company and do it with a thankful heart. Will you not speak to me?"

It gave him no reply. The hand was pointed straight before them.

"Lead on!" said Scrooge. "The night is waning fast, and it is precious time to me, I know."

The city seemed to spring up around them. There they were, in the heart of it, amongst the merchants who chinked the money in their pockets and conversed in groups. Scrooge had seen them often.

The Spirit stopped beside one knot of businessmen and pointed. Scrooge advanced to listen to their talk.

"I don't know much," said a man with a monstrous

chin. "I only know he died last night."

"Why, I thought he'd never die," said another.

"What has he done with his money?" asked a red-faced gentleman.

"I haven't heard," said the man with the large chin. "He hasn't left it to me. That's all I know."

This pleasantry was received with a general laugh.

"It's likely to be a very cheap funeral," said the same speaker, "for I don't know of anybody to go to it."

"I'll go if lunch is provided," observed the red-faced gentleman.

"I'll go, if anybody else will," said the first speaker. "When I come to think of it, I'm not sure that I wasn't his most particular friend, for we used to stop and speak whenever we met."

The group strolled away. Scrooge knew these men, and looked towards the Spirit for an explanation.

There was none.

Scrooge was at first surprised that the Spirit should attach importance to conversations so trivial, but feeling assured that they must have some hidden purpose, he considered what it was likely to be. He could not think of anyone connected with himself to whom he could apply them. But not doubting that they had some latent moral for his own improvement, he resolved to treasure up every word and everything he saw, and especially to observe the shadow of himself when it appeared. For he expected that the conduct of his future self would give him the clue he missed and render the solution of these riddles easy.

He looked about for his own image; but another man stood in his accustomed corner and he saw no likeness of himself among the multitudes.

The Phantom stood beside him with outstretched hand. Scrooge felt the unseen eyes were looking at him keenly. It made him shudder and feel very cold. They left the busy scene and went into an obscure part of town, where the ways were foul and narrow and the shops and houses wretched. The whole quarter reeked with crime, filth, and misery.

Far in this den of infamous resort there was a low-browed shop where iron, old rags, bottles, and refuse were bought. Upon the floor within were piled up heaps of rusty keys, nails, chains, hinges, files, scales, weights, and refuse iron of all kinds. Secrets that few would like to scrutinize were hidden in mountains of unseemly rubbish here. Sitting among the wares he dealt in, by a charcoal-stove made of old bricks, was a gray-haired rascal, Old Joe, who had screened himself from the cold air without and smoked his pipe in all the luxury of calm retirement.

Scrooge and the Phantom came into the presence of this person just as two women and a black-suited man came in, each carrying a bundle.

"Come into the parlor," Joe said to them.

The parlor was behind a screen of rags, a curtaining of miscellaneous tatters.

"Let's have a look," directed Joe, and the man, an undertaker's apprentice, came forward and produced his plunder. It was not extensive. A seal, a pencil case, a pair of sleeve buttons, and a cheap brooch. They were appraised by old Joe, who chalked the sums he was disposed to give for each upon the wall.

"That's your account," said Joe. "Nothing more. Who's next?"

Mrs. Dilber, the laundress, was next. Sheets and towels, some wearing apparel, two old-fashioned silver teaspoons, a few boots. Her account was stated on the wall in the same manner.

"And now undo my bundle, Joe," said the first woman.

Joe unwound the knots, and dragged out a heavy roll of some dark stuff.

"Bed curtains!" cried the woman, laughing.

"You don't mean to say you took 'em down, rings and all, with him lying there?" said Joe.

"Yes, I do," replied the woman. "Why not?"

"You were born to make your fortune," said Joe, "and you certainly will."

"I certainly shan't hold back my hand when I can get something by reaching out, for the sake of such a man as he was, I promise you," returned the woman coolly. Then she held up her prize.

"Look at this shirt till your eyes ache," she said. "You won't find a threadbare place. It's the best he had, and a fine one, too. They'd have wasted it, if it hadn't been for me."

"What do you call wasting it?" asked Joe.

"Somebody was fool enough to put it on him to be buried in," replied the woman with a laugh. "But I took it off again and changed to an old calico one, good enough for the purpose."

Scrooge listened to this dialogue in horror. As they sat grouped about their spoil, he viewed them with a detestation which could hardly have been greater if they had been demons, marketing the corpse itself.

"Ha, ha!" laughed the same woman, when Joe, producing a flannel bag of money, told out their several gains upon the ground.

"This is the end of it, you see. He frightened everyone away from him when he was alive," she said. "If he had somebody to look after him when he was struck with Death, instead of lying gasping out his last alone, we never would have had these things. But it's our profit, now he's dead. Everyone has a right to take care of themselves. He always did! Ha, Ha!"

"Spirit!" said Scrooge, shuddering from head to foot. "I see. The case of this unhappy man might be my own. My life tends that way, now. Merciful Heaven! What is this!"

He recoiled in terror, for the scene had changed, and now he almost touched a bed; a bare, uncurtained bed, on which beneath a ragged sheet, there lay a something covered up, which, though it was dumb, announced itself in awful language.

The room was dark, too dark to be observed with any accuracy, though Scrooge glanced round anxiously. A pale light fell upon the bed, and on it, plundered and bereft, unwatched, unwept, uncared for, was the body of this man.

Scrooge glanced towards the Phantom. Its steady hand was pointed to the head. The cover was so carelessly adjusted that the slightest raising of it, the motion of a finger upon Scrooge's part, would have disclosed the face. Scrooge longed to do it, but could not. He had no more power to withdraw that veil than to dismiss the specter at his side.

Still the Ghost pointed with an unmoved finger

to the head.

He lay, in the dark empty house, with not a man, a woman, or a child to say that he was kind to me in this or that, and for the memory of one kind word I will be kind to him. A cat was tearing at the door, and there was a sound of gnawing rats beneath the hearth stone. What they wanted in the room of death, and why they were so restless and disturbed, Scrooge did not dare to think.

"Spirit!" he said, "this is a fearful place. In leaving it, I shall not leave its lesson, trust me. Let us go!" Still the Ghost pointed with an unmoved finger to the head.

"I understand," Scrooge returned, "and I would do it, if I could. But I have not the power, Spirit." Again it seemed to look upon him.

"If there is any person in the town who feels emotion caused by this man's death," said Scrooge quite agonized, "show that person to me, Spirit, I beseech you!"

The Phantom spread its dark robe before him and withdrawing it, revealed a room by daylight, where a mother and her children were.

She was expecting someone with anxious eagerness, for she paced the room and glanced at the clock.

At length, the long-expected knock was heard. She hurried to meet her husband, a man whose face was care-worn and depressed, though he was young. There was a remarkable expression in it now, a kind of serious delight of which he felt ashamed and struggled to repress.

He sat down to his dinner and she asked him

faintly, what news. He appeared embarrassed how to answer.

"Bad," he answered.

"We are quite ruined?"

"No. There is hope yet, Caroline."

"If he relents," she said, amazed, "there is! Nothing is past hope, if such a miracle has happened."

"He is dead," said her husband.

She was a patient creature if her face spoke truth, but she was thankful in her soul to hear it, and she said so, with clasped hands. She prayed forgiveness the next moment and was sorry, but the first was the emotion of her heart.

"To whom will our debt be transferred?" she asked.

"I don't know. But before that time, we shall be ready with the money. And even if we were not, it would be unlikely to find so merciless a creditor in his successor. We may sleep tonight with light hearts, Caroline!"

Yes, their hearts were lighter and it was a happier house for this man's death! The only emotion that the Ghost could show him caused by the event was one of pleasure.

"Let me see some tenderness connected with a death," said Scrooge, "or that dark chamber, Spirit, which we left just now, will be forever present to me."

The Ghost conducted him through familiar streets, and as they went along, Scrooge looked here and there to find himself, but nowhere was he to be seen. They entered poor Bob Cratchit's house and found the mother and the children seated round the fire.

Quiet. Very quiet. The noisy little Cratchits were as still as statues and sat looking at Peter, who had a book before him. The mother and her daughters were sewing.

"And He took a child, and set him in the midst of them."

Where had Scrooge heard those words? The boy must have read them, as he and the Spirit entered.

The mother laid down her work and put her hand up to her face.

"The color hurts my eyes," she said.

The color? Ah, poor Tiny Tim!

"They're better now," said Cratchit's wife. "I wouldn't show weak eyes to your father when he comes home. He's late tonight."

"He's walked slower these few last evenings," Peter said.

They became very quiet again. At last she said, in a steady, cheerful voice that only faltered once: "He has walked with, he walked with Tiny Tim upon his shoulder, fast indeed. But he was very light to carry, and his father loved him so, that it was no trouble. And there is your father at the door!"

Bob, poor fellow, came in. They all rushed to greet him. The two young Cratchits got upon his knees and leaned against him as if to say, "Don't mind it, Father. Don't be grieved!"

Bob was very cheerful with them. He looked at the sewing and praised the industry and speed of Mrs. Cratchit. They would be done long before Sunday, he said.

"Sunday! You went today, then, Robert?" said his wife.

"Yes, dear," returned Bob. "I wish you could

have gone. But you'll see it often. I promised him that I would walk there on a Sunday. My little, little child! " cried Bob. "My little child! "

He broke down all at once. He couldn't help it.

He went upstairs into the room above which was lighted cheerfully and hung with Christmas. There was a chair set close beside the child, and poor Bob sat down. When he had thought a little and composed himself, he kissed the little face. He was reconciled to what had happened, and went down again quite happy.

They drew about the fire and talked. Bob told them of the extraordinary kindness of Mr. Scrooge's nephew, whom he had scarcely seen but once, and who, meeting him in the street, had said, "I am heartily sorry for it, Mr. Cratchit. If I can be of any service to you, pray, come to me. "

Then Bob Cratchit spoke to his family with earnestness.

"You will all be growing up and on your own some day, " he said. "But I am sure we shall none of us forget poor Tiny Tim, shall we? "

"Never, Father! " cried they all.

"I am very happy, " said Bob.

Mrs. Cratchit kissed him, his daughters kissed him, the two young Cratchits kissed him, and Peter and himself shook hands. Spirit of Tiny Tim, thy childish essence was from God!

"Specter, " said Scrooge, "something informs me that our parting moment is at hand. Tell me what man that was whom we saw lying dead? "

The Ghost of Christmas Yet to Come conveyed him to an iron gate. A church-yard. Here, then, the wretched man whose name he had now to learn lay underneath the ground. It was a worthy place. Walled in by houses, overrun by grass and weeds, the growth of vegetation's death, not life, choked up with too much burying, fat with repleted appetite. A worthy place!

The Spirit stood among the graves and pointed down to one.

"Before I draw nearer to that stone, " said Scrooge, "answer me one question. Are these the shadows of the things that will be, or are they shadows of things that may be, only? "

The Ghost pointed still.

"Men's courses will foreshadow certain ends, " said Scrooge. "But if the courses be departed from, the ends will change. Say it is thus with what you show me! "

The Spirit was immovable as ever.

Scrooge crept towards it, trembling and following the finger, read upon the stone of the neglected grave his own name, EBENEZER SCROOGE.

"Am I that man whose death I have heard of tonight? " he cried, upon his knees.

The finger pointed from the grave to him, and back again.

"No, Spirit! Oh, no, no! "

"Spirit! " he cried. "Hear me! I am not the man I was. Why show me this, if I am past all hope! " For the first time the hand appeared to shake.

"Good Spirit, " he pursued, "assure me that I yet may change these shadows you have shown me, by an altered life! "

The kind hand trembled.

"I will honor Christmas in my heart, and try to keep it all the year. I will not shut out the lessons of the Past, Present, and Future. Oh, tell me I may sponge away the writing on this stone!"

In his agony, he caught the spectral hand. It sought to free itself, but he was strong in his entreaty. The Spirit, stronger yet, repulsed him.

Holding up his hands in a last prayer to have his fate reversed, he saw an alteration in the Phantom's hood and dress. It shrunk, collapsed, and dwindled down into a bedpost.

CHAPTER FIVE

Yes! And the bedpost was his own. The bed was his own, the room was his own. Best and happiest of all, the time before him was his own, to make amends in!

"I will live in the Past, the Present, and the Future!" Scrooge repeated, as he scrambled out of bed. "The Spirits of all three shall strive within me. Oh, Jacob Marley! Heaven, and the Christmas time be praised for this! I say it on my knees, old Jacob!"

He was so fluttered with his good intentions, that he could barely speak. He had been sobbing violently in the conflict with the Spirit, and his face was wet with tears.

"They are not torn down," cried Scrooge, folding one of his bed curtains in his arms. "They are here. I am here. The shadows of the things that would have been may be dispelled. They will be! I know they will!"

His agitation was so great he hopped about putting his clothes on inside out and upside down.

"I don't know what to do!" cried Scrooge, laughing and crying in the same breath. "I am light as a feather. Happy as an angel. Merry as a school boy. A Merry Christmas to everybody! Hallo! Whoop! Hallo!"

"There's the saucepan the gruel was in!" cried Scrooge, frisking round the fireplace. "There's the door by which the Ghost of Jacob Marley entered! There's the corner whence the Ghost of Christmas Present sat! It all happened. Ha, ha, ha!"

For a man who had been out of practice for so many years, it was a splendid laugh.

"I don't know what day of the month it is!" said Scrooge. "I don't know how long I've been among the Spirits. I'm quite a baby. Never mind. I don't care. Whoop! Hallo there!"

He was checked in his transports by the churches ringing out the lustiest peals he had ever heard. Clash, clang, hammer, ding, dong, bell. Bell, dong, ding, hammer, clang, clash! Oh, glorious, glorious! Running to the window, he opened it and put out his head. No fog—clear, stirring cold. Golden sunlight, sweet air. Glorious!

"What's today?" cried Scrooge, calling down to a boy below.

"Today!" replied the boy. "Why, CHRISTMAS DAY."

"It's Christmas Day!" said Scrooge to himself. "I haven't missed it. The Spirits have done it all in one night. Of course, they can do anything they like."

"Hallo!" he called to the boy. "Do you know the poulterer's on the corner?"

"I should hope I did," replied the lad.

"An intelligent boy!" said Scrooge. "Do you know whether they've sold the prize turkey that was hanging there?"

"It's hanging there now," replied the boy.

"Go and buy it for me," said Scrooge. "Tell 'em to bring it here, so I may give them directions where to take it. Come back with the man and I'll give you a shilling. Come back in less than five minutes and I'll give you half a crown!"

The boy was off like a shot.

"I'll send it to Bob Cratchit's!" whispered Scrooge, laughing. "He shan't know who sends it. It's twice the size of Tiny Tim!"

The hand in which he wrote the address was not a steady one, but write it he did, and went downstairs to wait for the poulterer's man. As he stood there, the knocker caught his eye.

"I shall love it, as long as I live!" cried Scrooge, patting it with his hand. "I never looked at it before. What an honest expression it has in its face! Hallow! Here's the turkey, Merry Christmas!"

It was a turkey! He never could have stood upon his legs, that bird. He would have snapped 'em short off in a minute, like sticks of sealing wax.

"Why, it's impossible to carry that to Cratchit's," said Scrooge. "You must have a cab."

The chuckles with which he paid for the turkey, and the chuckle with which he paid for the cab, and

the chuckle with which he recompensed the boy, were only exceeded by the chuckle with which he sat down breathless in his chair again and cried.

He dressed himself "all in his best" and went out into the streets. The people were pouring forth as he had seen them with the Ghost of Christmas Present. Walking with his hands behind him, Scrooge regarded everyone with a delighted smile.

He had not gone far, when he beheld the gentleman who had walked into his counting-house the day before and said, "Scrooge and Marley's, I believe?"

"Dear sir," Scrooge said, taking the gentleman by both his hands. "I hope you succeeded yesterday. A Merry Christmas to you!"

"Mr. Scrooge?"

"Yes," said Scrooge. "Allow me to ask your pardon. And will you have the goodness . . ." Here Scrooge whispered in his ear.

"My dear Mr. Scrooge," cried the gentleman, "are you serious?"

"Not a farthing less," said Scrooge. "A great many back payments are included in it, I assure you."

"I don't know what to say to such munifi—" said the other, shaking his head.

"Don't say anything," Scrooge returned. "I am obliged to you. Bless you!"

He went to church and walked about the streets. He watched people hurrying about, and patted children on the head. He had never dreamed that any walk—that anything—could give him so much happiness. In the afternoon, he turned towards his nephew's house.

He passed the door a dozen times before he had the courage to knock. But knock he did.

"Is your master home?" said Scrooge to the girl. Nice girl!

"Yes, sir," she answered. "He's in the dining room along with mistress. I'll show you in."

"Thank'ee. He knows me," said Scrooge, with his hand already on the dining room lock. "I'll go in here."

He turned it gently and sidled his face in, round the door.

"Fred!" said Scrooge.

"Why bless my soul!" cried Fred, "Who's that?"

"It's I. Your uncle Scrooge. I have come to dinner. Will you let me in, Fred?"

My, how his niece by marriage started!

Let him in! It is a mercy he didn't shake his arm off. He was at home in five minutes. Wonderful party, wonderful games, won-der-ful happiness!

But he was early at the office next morning. If he could only be there first and catch Bob Cratchit coming late! That was what he had set his heart upon.

And he did it. The clock struck nine. No Bob. He was full eighteen minutes behind his time. Scrooge sat with his door open, so he might see him come into the tank.

Poor Bob was in the door and on his stool in a jiffy, driving away with his pen.

"Hallo!" growled Scrooge, in his accustomed voice. "What do you mean by coming here at this time?"

"I am very sorry, sir," pleaded Bob. "It's only once a year, sir. It shall not be repeated. I was making

rather merry yesterday."

"I'll tell you what, my friend," said Scrooge. "I am not going to stand this sort of thing any longer. And therefore . . ." he continued, leaping from his stool, "I am about to raise your salary!"

Bob trembled and got a little nearer to the ruler. He had a momentary idea of knocking Scrooge down with it; holding him up, and calling people in the court for help and a straight-jacket.

"A Merry Christmas, Bob!" said Scrooge, with an earnestness that could not be mistaken, as he clapped him on the back. "A Merrier Christmas than I have given you for many a year! I'll raise your salary, and endeavor to assist your struggling family, Bob! Make up the fires, and buy another coal scuttle before you dot another 'i', Bob Cratchit!"

Scrooge was better than his word. He did it all, and infinitely more. And to Tiny Tim, who did *not* die, he was a second father. He became as good a friend, as good a master, and as good a man as the good old city knew. Some people laughed to see the alteration in him, but he let them laugh, and little heeded them. His own heart laughed, and that was quite enough for him.

He had no further intercourse with Spirits. And it was always said of him that he knew how to keep Christmas well, if any man alive possessed the knowledge. May that be truly said of us, and all of us! And so, as Tiny Tim observed, "God bless us, every one!"